For Franny, Lilly, and Maria—
Welcome!

Library of Congress catalog card number: 93-10093
Published simultaneously in Canada by HarperCollins*CanadaLtd*
Color separations by Vimnice
Printed and bound in the United States of America
by Worzalla
First edition, 1993

The Family Reunion
Tricia Tusa

FARRAR · STRAUS · GIROUX

NEW YORK

It was the annual Beneada family reunion.
Almost everyone had arrived.

The soda was full of fizz.
The chips were nice and crispy.

Uncle Phil was finishing up his famous imitation
of a rock when the front door opened.

The couple standing there didn't look at all familiar.

Who were they? Nobody seemed to know.

Little Luther shouted, "Hey! Who are you?"

How embarrassing! He was hushed immediately.

Cousin Eloise was more tactful.
    "Welcome! It's been so long—too long! How
nice of you to bring refreshments. Won't you
come on over here and fill out name tags?"

Esther and Fester!

Oh, of course, Esther and Fester!

Who in the world were Esther and Fester?

The group politely excused itself

and met in the kitchen.

"How are we related to these people?" asked Aunt Nana.

"Ah, yes! I remember. Talented cousin Esther and Uncle Fester—

from the circus!" said nephew Walt.

"Of course!" they all exclaimed as they cartwheeled and back-flipped out to the den.

They did what they could to put their circus relatives at ease.
Fester was encouraged to join in the juggling, and Esther to try out the trapeze.
The vegetables ended up on the carpet. So did Esther.

Everybody was back for a meeting.

"Clearly, these are not our cousins from the circus."

"Oh, dear, who could they be?" they all wondered.

Minutes passed before sister Sally said, "Surely they're not our *famous* cousins Esther and Fester."

"The makers of Dinky Donuts?" asked Lenore.

"Yes, yes! The ones on TV!" answered Sam.

Everyone did his or her best doughnut and sang the
"I-want-to-be-a-Dinky-Donut, can't-you-see" jingle.
Esther and Fester did not join in.

This could not be Esther and Fester, the doughnut enthusiasts.
Who were they?

After much discussion, it was unanimously decided they were
niece Esther and her husband, Fester,

both doctors and world-renowned for pioneering work
in their field of specialty, belly buttons.

While everyone lined up, waiting for a consultation,
Aunt Carolyn suddenly gasped for air and fainted.

Once revived, she whispered in horror, "I know who those people are. I recognize their profiles. They're our *distant* cousins Esther and Fester . . ." She fainted again.

But Uncle Dan went on, ". . . who were given a life sentence in the state pen!" He fainted.

"They've escaped!" shrieked Luther.

Everyone ran screaming into the den, hiding
themselves as best they could. Esther and Fester
began to scream as well,

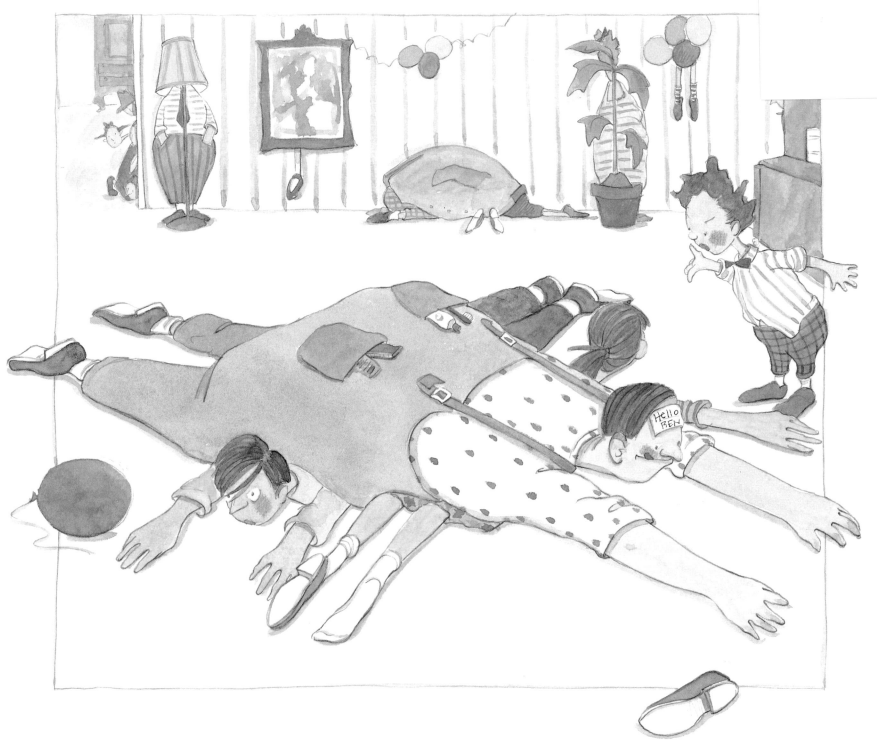

especially when tackled by Brother Ben.

Luther, very bravely, approached the criminals.

"Who do you think you are?!"

After some coughing and sputtering, Fester said, "Uh, pardon me, but we were wondering the same thing about you. We'd be happy to introduce ourselves, if you would kindly do the same. My name is Fester Jones. This is my wife, Esther Jones."

"Esther and Fester Jones!" blurted Aunt Bev. "We aren't related to you! *What* are you doing here—eating our chips?"

"These are *our* chips. This is *our* house," explained Esther.

"We just went out for a few minutes to the grocery store and came back to . . ."

Little Luther pulled out the party invitation. "Isn't this 239 Rosebud Lane?"

"No," said Esther. "This is 236 Rosebud Lane."

Grandpa Sam blew his whistle and announced, "Wrong house, team!"

And they were gone.

Chips and all.

"Hey, hey, hey! The gang's all here.
Sorry we're late!"